LITTLE ABODE FOR CHILDREN

A MYSTERY

SANHITA MUKHERJEE

Made with ♥ on the Notion Press Platform
www.notionpress.com

The Redears

Contents

CHAPTER ONE

The Library

Kenosha public library was the milieu of the people from all hues of life. It harbored homeless people, newly arrived at the town along with the well-to-do residents of its older neighborhoods around the library and library park. The older patrons of the library used to seek entertainment and socializing opportunities at the library. The other group used the library as an information and learning hub.

It was an early spring evening. The neoclassical architecture of the library building seemed scintillating from bright lights reflected from grasses, sprouting leaves and inflorescence of large trees of the surrounding rectangular park, known as Library Park. Inside, it was full of different activity groups occupying different corners. Toddlers were busy with stories of flowers and insects. By this group was a cluster of members from Kenosha Knitting Circle, comprising grown and elderly men and women. The toddlers were keener on chasing bright and colorful balls of woolen yarns than giving an ear to the stories.

Middle and high school students were thronging here and there. Some were volunteering with the library. Their friends were just hanging around them. Some were doing their projects very seriously, scattered mostly around the reference section, history, geography science and literature sections.

Tanya and Asia screamed suddenly. They were standing in between the aisles of classic literature. Their friends rushed to them. They also screamed. Lisa, that evening's student coordinator for the library, rushed to the screaming youngsters. She, too, shrieked. Her supervisor Mrs. Henkel was with the Knitting Circle. She went to the aisles of screams. Then, she called Detective Nathan Adams of Kenosha Police Department. Detective Adams was working alone because half of the Police Department was in quarantine then. His partner belonged to that half.

By the time Detective Adams arrived at the library, both the groups of haves and have-nots gathered around the classic literature section. The older group was occupied appeasing the young ones. Teressa LeRoy's gown startled everybody. The gown was hanging from the shelves of the classics in the literature section. Teressa wore it on the night of the gala. Nobody had seen her after that night.

CHAPTER TWO

Teressa LeRoy

Teressa used to live alone. She was one of the student coordinators of the library. She did not show up for work on the day after the gala. Nor did she call in sick. It was very unlikely of her.

Mrs. Henkel, Teressa's supervisor, tried to call her when she remained absent at work another day consecutively. Mrs. Henkel's calls ended up repeatedly at voice mail. Worried, Mrs. Henkel, on the day after, while coming to work, stopped by Teressa's apartment to check on her. It was locked and nobody answered her knock on the door. Mrs. Henkel reported the matter to the police. That day during the afternoon, Detective Nathan Adams showed up in the library. He asked Mrs. Henkel a lot of questions.

Mrs. Henkel was all praise for Teressa. According to Mrs. Henkel, Teressa was a dedicated library worker. She brought up neighborhood children to the library for several summer projects and events. These children were not only from wealthy and working-class households of the neighborhood, but also from the streets around the Metra Station, Simmons Park, Harbor Park and all other public places of the city.

Nathan was compelled to talk to the children. The children were very depressed. They were missing Teressa very much. She had not only brought them to the library, but also she helped them with their homework, school projects and other studies. Especially to the street kids, she was a tutor and a mentor. Apparently, Teressa was only loved and admired; she had no enemy.

After a day of toil, Nathan had no clue about the disappearance of Teressa Leroy. So, he started revisiting his notes.

CHAPTER THREE

The Gala

The gala was for raising funds for building up a shelter for the street children. Kenosha did not yet have any.

City's older generation had always been generous to these children. They used to take these children for fostering. One among the foster parents was Mrs. Kirk.

Mrs. Kirk used to teach History at Kenosha Middle School. She retired a few years ago. A year ago, she suffered from her first heart attack. It shook her thoughts about the children she used to look after. Since then she started thinking of building a home for street kids. After all, these children could never be sent back. She expressed this concern of her to her friends at Kenosha Knitting Circle.

Mrs. Mary Munro was in the circle. She was Teressa's grand aunt. She knew about Teressa's involvement and effort with the children. She shared, "My grandniece, Teressa, runs a center for the street kids. Off course with help and support from her friends and family. She, too, needs an expansion. Can we talk to her?"

Hence, Teressa with Kenosha Knitting Circle arranged a fundraiser event for expansion of Little Abode for Children. The library supported the event by hosting the gala on the first floor of the library building.

The gala appeared to be quite a success. It helped gather a million dollar in contribution. Kenosha Undergarment Factory, a leading global manufacturer of underwear, donated one of their abandoned warehouses to build a kitchen and shelter for rescued street children.

Nathan scribbled a question in his notebook, "Who'd be against such benevolent endeavors and enthusiasts?"

CHAPTER FOUR

The Children

The children were mostly from Chicago. A few of them were from Milwaukee. The railroads carried them to Kenosha, the picturesque town by the lake Michigan.

Coming from North or South, their stories were almost the same. All of them either escaped a terrible home or fled from a dangerous neighborhood. Many of them had at least one parent in jail. Many of them used to be beaten to bleed either by a harsh stepparent, or by an aggressive stepsibling, or by a drug addict half sibling, or by a gang banger cousin. Some escaped schools as gangs started using schools for gang initiation.

Many of them found a safe home with Mrs. Kirk and other members of Kenosha Knitting Circle, like Teressa's Aunt Mary. They found hope in learning and joy in living at gracious foster homes. For them, the library was their gateway to the universe of knowledge.

After Teressa's disappearance, they used to gather at the library to help each other learn. It was their way of paying respect to Teressa.

CHAPTER FIVE

The Ghost

Keith and Melissa were living with Mrs. Owen. Mrs. Owen used to teach ballet at her own studio at Kenosha downtown. She was also a member of Kenosha Knitting Circle.

Keith was assigned a project by his History teacher about industries of Kenosha before the Second World War. Mrs. Owen had many books about dances, arts and culture in her personal collection, but those were of no help to Keith.

Social distancing and lockdown due to the coronavirus outbreak shortened the library hours since the day after Ms. LeRoy's gown appeared in the library. The library's digital repository was not much open to the children under eighteen. Mrs. Henkel or the librarian, Mrs. Atkins, like earlier, could no longer override the VPN access password for the children, if they thought fit. Borrowing Kindle, for accessing digital resources, seemed impossible, too.

After much discussion, Keith and Melissa found themselves desperate to access the library for at least one half of a day. They cooked a plan.

They entered the library during its opening hours, then sneaked into the library reference section, remained hidden there till the library was closed for the public and all the staff left. They had planned to surrender to the janitor at night, making an apology for being locked inside, reasoning that they were working in rapt attention oblivious of the library closing time, and expressing surprises for not being noticed by the library staff before closing of the library.

They were almost done by late evening. Their ears were up to hear the janitor entering the library. Their work was being disrupted intermittently by lights being turned off by the motion sensors. To keep them on, Melissa was strolling around the table where Keith was working.

She saw a woman roaming in the history section of the library. She whispered to Keith. Together they approached the history section to get a closer peek at her. The lights along their path were turning on as they proceeded.

Suddenly, all the lights turned off, altogether. Moving to and fro, Keith and Melissa were confirmed that the motion sensors had stopped working. Trapped in darkness, they lost direction.

They had heard the rumor that Ms. LeRoy could have died inside the library and her ghost could have remained confined thereof. Especially, many guessed that her ghost had hung the gown in the classic literature section.

The ghost hypothesis sparked first into Keith's mind. He muttered it to Melissa. They turned numb in horror. Then, using flashlights of cell phones, they crawled to an emergency exit.

As soon as their feet touched the grounds of Library Park, they started running towards the nearest streetlights. As they opened the emergency exit, the library's electronic security system raised the alarm.

Nathan heard the alarm. He was in Library Park, measuring the times required to reach any of the drivable roads around Library Park from the library building. He ran towards the library building to check for break ins before patrol cars appeared. Keith and Melissa ran into him.

He took them to a nearby Waffle House. After sipping some hot chocolate, Melissa got her colors back. Keith was still panting. By and by, they spilled their plan to Nathan and how it went sideways.

Nathan noted, "Keith and Melissa were escaping a ghost in the library! Must pay a visit to this ghost."

CHAPTER SIX

The Streets

Nathan was walking from Seventh Avenue towards the library building. He was remembering that the library neighborhood used to be one of the safest areas in the city. Yet it appeared to be a high crime area compared to neighborhoods far west from the lake.

These thoughts brought into his mind what he had read once in a police training material. Statistically high crime rates were observed within walking distance from public transit stations.

From Kenosha Metra Station, the library was just fifteen minutes' walk along eleventh avenue and sixtieth street, across eighth street. He could not help but blame Metra Station and its link to Chicago for the general high crime rates of the city. Kenosha appeared in several studies for its higher crime rates compared to other cities of similar size and population in the nation.

He walked past the entire Library Park and arrived at the brink of Eighth Avenue. He needed darkness to pursue the ghost in the library. Hence, he ventured to walking to Metra Station and walking back to the library when it was dark. He had also decided to reconnoiter the southwest corner of Library Park. This corner appeared to be the fringe area of high crime zones in the city.

The pleasant summer breeze brought a shadow of loneliness. It reminded Nathan of his friends. Some of them went back to school in pursuit of advanced business degrees or law degrees. Nathan chose police work, after leaving active service in the military.

Returning from his second tour to Afghanistan he discovered that his mother had become older and frailer. He wished to live near her. She suggested Nathan join the police force like his father. That was five years ago.

Since then he has become somewhat submerged in work. He barely found time to meet new people outside work. In the past five years, he has not made any friends. Nor did he go on any date.

Around Metra Station, he found a few children loitering about. Some were in hoodies and pretended to walk fast to a defined destination. Nathan walked further North and came back to the station in a while, just to check that children who pretended to walk away were back in the waiting area.

Nathan felt sorry for the children. The evening pleasantness brought by the breeze would turn to chill during the wee hours of the day. The children would suffer in the cold until the child services department would rescue them.

He was thinking of calling the child services department. He was hesitating because the call might shift his focus from the job in hand.

By that time, a colorfully painted van appeared, displaying the name Little Abode for Children, on its flanks. A young woman along with an old woman stepped out of the van. They interacted with the children and all the children boarded the van. Nathan made a note about the event.

He visited Little Abode for Children the very next day. It was linked to the missing woman, Teressa LeRoy. At the office and shelter of Little Abode for Children Nathan was received by Samantha. She used to volunteer there thrice a week. For a paid job, she used to work at Grand Electricals and Finances based at Milwaukee. Her husband used to be an engineer, with Kenosha City Council. They had three children together.

Samantha told Nathan, “It was Teressa’s brainchild. She used to be here before going to work for the library five days a week and after her shift at the library is over. She is, was, the heart of the center. First kid she rescued on a wintry night was Melissa. Teressa was herself a student then. Her elder sister, Ellen, works for the city Child Services Department. The two sisters partnered in this endeavor. Later, their entire family and extended family, friends joined hands. We even had a gala ..... Everything has changed that night. The children are still reeling in shock. Jack has stopped stepping outside home. He probably feels guilty.”

The story of creating Little Abode for Children filled Nathan’s heart with warmth. He enrolled to be a volunteer.

However, Nathan needed to know more about Jack. Hence, he asked Samantha about Jack’s address. Jack was then living with Mrs. Kirk.

CHAPTER SEVEN

The Body

Almost a week has passed since the gala night. Captain Brown called Nathan and enquired, "What's the problem? Haven't you searched the library thoroughly?"

Nathan replied, "I did Ma'am. In fact, I have found some leads. I mentioned them in detail in my updated report. We still need to protect certain persons like Jack O'hara till we can make the necessary arrests."

Captain Brown seemed impatient, "When have you updated your report?

Nathan answered, "Last night."

Captain seemed to be browsing through the report on the computer screen in front of her. She tightened her jaws and commented, "Have you filed for permission to access the feeds from surveillance cameras already?"

Nathan became enthusiastic in his response, "Yes, I have copied necessary clips from traffic camera footage. Metra Station footage is about to arrive. Only, Judge Hopkins is waiting for the opinion of Kenosha county officials since they manage Simmons Public Library. The gala was a private event. If the county would have waived its privilege of surveillance over the library premises during the event, then Judge Hopkins may be required to subpoena financial details of donations of the gala night from the organizers, especially, Little Abode for Children, and, also, their video recordings of the event. However, I have asked Little Abode for Children for their guest list for the gala night. They have provided the list."

Lieutenant Kelly entered the captain's office. He reported, "Captain, we've got a mangled body on the steps of the arena around the war memorial in Library Park ..."

Captain Brown frowned and murmured, "Due North of the library building." And asked, "Who's reported?"

Lieutenant Kelly answered, "A jogger. By a nine one one call."

Detective Nathan was on his feet already. He asked for permission, "Can I attend the crime scene, Captain, Lieutenant?"

Obviously, he was permitted.

At the crime scene Coroner Goodman was still in action. She looked up and nodded to Detective Nathan Adams. Nathan smiled and asked, "What does the good doctor have here for me?"

Dr. Goodman reported, "A woman. Mid-thirties. Died primarily of asphyxiation. Dark discoloration of the skin at places, cyanosis .... pointing to asphyxiation. Unless I do the X-rays I can barely tell what has caused the asphyxia. Also, the disfigurement of face and fingers, require me to study a little more to determine if those mangling occurred before her death or after. Time of death is between one to three in the morning today."

City news mill started brewing if the body belonged to Teressa LeRoy. Captain Brown called the press and announced, "From primary investigations it appears that the bodily remains of a human female found in Library Park does not belong to Ms. LeRoy. At this time, we cannot share any update about any of the ongoing investigations about Ms. LeRoy's disappearance or about the dead body discovered at Library Park."

Nathan rushed to meet Teressa LeRoy's sister Ellen and Aunt Mary. Nathan felt quite familiar to them. He appeased them, "You must trust me. Teressa is well and alive. As soon as we take the person responsible for her disappearance in custody, she will probably be able to call you."

From looks on their respective faces Nathan guessed that none of them believed Nathan's statement. Yet he refrained from being more convincing for the sake of the investigation.

CHAPTER EIGHT

Chicago or Milwaukee

Nathan was already investigating Ms. LeRoy's disappearance from the library. Teressa LeRoy was twenty-seven. Now this thirtysomething woman's dead body, too, appeared in Library Park. Hence, the investigation about the latter woman was assigned to him.

Nathan went to the coroner's office in the morning. Dr. Goodman was ready with the report. She explained, "It's murder. The victim was indeed asphyxiated. Absence of ligature marks on her neck though contradicts the fact of asphyxiation... also, the x-rays showing no damage to her windpipe ..... yet .... Her broken rib ... especially, rib bones four and seven pierced into her lungs. Both right and left lungs were punctured. Hence, she was asphyxiated."

Nathan had to know, hence asked, "Disfigurements? Of fingers? And the face?"

Dr. Goodman explained, "From huge blood coagulations around ruptured tissues, it is obvious that disfigurements were caused to her before she died. Pulled out nails, charred fingertips indicate that she was tortured. Then she was killed. The breaking of rib bones was too due to torture. Probably the perpetrators could not fathom that their victim would be dead before they would let her die. Hence, they dumped the body as soon as they could."

Nathan needed more, "What about the DNA?"

Dr. Goodman smiled and reminded, "Latest by tomorrow .... I'm expecting to get the DNA analysis results later tonight."

X-ray analysis of the victim induced in Nathan an instinctive rush for obtaining all surveillance footage around Library Park and Metra Station. Hence, his next stop was the District Attorney's office.

Nathan was thinking fast. The perpetrators might drive from Chicago to Kenosha to dump the body at Library Park. Otherwise, they might be staying at Kenosha. If perpetrators were aware of Jack living in Kenosha, they would try penetrating into Little Abode for children and would find Jack in the foster children's network.

Around afternoon he reported everything to Captain Brown. She suggested, "Why are you only looking into Chicago? Why not Milwaukee? Metra Station can be a spot for gathering for anyone living in, coming to Kenosha."

Nathan shared, "I've checked with both the police departments at Chicago and Milwaukee. Chicago PD reported that one Susan Crawford disappeared from Chicago on the same night as Teressa. When I interviewed children from Chicago rescued by Little Abode for Children and living in different foster homes around Kenosha, Jack O'hara mentioned that he had invited Ms. Crawford to the gala."

Nathan also added, "In the interview Jack reported, 'Ms. Crawford is a witness in the murder case of my elder brother Joe. The Meatloaf gang was trying to recruit seniors in Joe's school. They killed our parents to make Joe join them. Sensing the situation, Ms. Crawford tried to ship us brothers off Chicago. She brought me from my school and bought me the ticket to Kenosha and asked me to wait for the city Child Services Department at Metra Station. She learnt about it from the Facebook page of Little Abode for Children. But she couldn't rescue Joe. To terrorize other kids in the school and to show them how horrific could be a denial to gang recruitment, they hacked Joe to death. Ms. Crawford found Joe's mangled body at the school football ground.' Since then Ms. Crawford was living under police protection pending her testimony in the court."

Next Nathan met the head of the city Child Services department. He explained, "Jack is vulnerable to attack by some criminals. We need to shift him to police custody. Please, allow me to keep him in my home."

But the department policy was against unmarried men or women below the age of forty fostering children. Nathan explained the situation to Captain Brown. She took custody of Jack. She was married to another detective. Their son was almost the same age as Jack.

CHAPTER NINE

Detective's Night Adventure

In the evening, Nathan was telling a ghost story to the children at Little Abode for Children shelter. He was trying not to smile. This particular story brought him happiness. It even made his mother happy. He was in love with the story.

He continued, "K and M, two siblings saw a ghost in the library. They were scared. They somehow reached one of the emergency exits of the library building and left. Their exit turned on the library security alarm. They were in the library after its closure and, thus, broke the rules. Hence, they were trying to avoid the police. In the dark of the night, running through Library Park, they simply fall upon Detective D. Detective D was trying to figure out a murder in the park. As K and M told him about the ghost, next night he entered the library by using his police key. Searching all floors Detective D found a bedroll spread on the floor in the attic of the library. No motion sensors were working there. A table lamp was on, by the bedroll, illuminating a stack of books. He started watching the bedroll, book and the lamp stealthily from behind an old mahogany chest of drawers. Suddenly, in the sea of silence, he heard someone breathing on his neck. He was sure that it was not a ghost. Ghosts can't breathe because they are dead people. When people die, they usually stop breathing."

At this point, Natalie commented, "Gross."

Others screamed, "What happened next?"

Nathan continued, "Detective D was swift. As he was turning back, the person behind him kicked on his knees from the back. Adjusting balance to prevent a fall, D turned around completely and received a blow on his nose, by a heavy book. Yet he smiled. For he found someone he was looking for some time. He had seen her photos. He heard a lot of good things about her. Until the blow on the nose he never realized that he fell in love with the missing person. So, he prayed on his knees, 'Will you marry me?' The missing person said 'Yes.' Then they lived happily ever after."

Patrick commented, "You're a terrible storyteller."

Nathan did not notice Lisa was standing by the door. She came to stay with the children that night. She asked eerily, "Have you found Teressa?"

Nathan was not sure if he blushed. He had uttered a rehearsed answer to this question too many times. Hence, he confidently replied, "Not yet. The investigation is on."

From Lisa's countenance he gathered that Lisa was swallowing trails of questions and judgements, like, "Are you in love with the victim in one of your cases?", "Is that a way to talk about a missing person?", "This' gross, man."

Later in the evening, Dr. Goodman called Nathan and informed, "DNA is a match. The victim was Ms. Susan Crawford of Chicago."

CHAPTER TEN

Another Boy from Chicago

Following day Captain Brown asked, "Are you done with the footage?"

Nathan replied, "Almost. It's sure that the van that dropped Ms. Crawford's body was from Chicago. Its license plate is still in active registration. Only the passengers could not be identified properly because of the face masks. Those weren't worn to prevent viral contamination of COVID-19. But those were masks used in burglaries, bank robberies."

Captain Brown mentioned, "Jack has identified the Meatloaf members, Tony, Timothy and Miranda. From the footage of the gala night. Also, he exclaimed that Ms. Crawford left the party in Ms. LeRoy's outfit and vice versa. Do you know anything about it, Adams?"

Before Nathan could answer, Lieutenant Kelly interrupted, "Pardon me Captain. Got a call about an abandoned warehouse on Seventy fifth street near Kenosha Business Park, with lots of blood, discovered and reported by the property manager while she was checking it before handing it over to a new tenant. We presume the warehouse being the primary crime scene in Susan Crawford's murder. We've sent the blood samples to the lab. As soon as we get the results, we'll inform you and Detective Adams."

Nathan added hurriedly, "From other footage from the library, I saw a female teenager, hanging the gown from the library shelf. I showed a photo of the female to several children. Most of them told that she was asking around about Jack O'hara while in the library. To some of the children, the female identified herself as Miranda."

In the evening, at Little Abode for Children shelter, Nathan met Jeremy. Nathan knew from the footage of the day that Jeremy did not come to the station by Metra train, like other children. Rather, he came from a motel on seventy fifth street.

Jeremy asked everyone at the center, "Do you know where Jack lives? I miss him. He's my best friend. I'd like to meet him."

Nathan replied, "What's the rush? You're now going to live here till you graduate from high school and learn a trade. You'll meet Jack, anyway. This' a small city."

Then Nathan texted Captain Brown, "Please ask Jack to make his Facebook page live. Tonight's the night."

Then he received a text message from Lieutenant Kelly, "The blood sample matches the DNA of Susan Crawford. Also, traces of it match DNA of Timothy Cooke, Anthony Parsons, Jeremy Wilson and Miranda Boyd."

Later in the night, a police raid led by Lieutenant Kelly on Pine Ridge Motel on seventy fifth street nabbed Timothy Cooke alias Tim, Anthony Parsons alias Tony and Miranda Boyd. Nathan was there.

Around the same time, Captain Brown's home was invaded by someone. As that person entered the dark bedroom mentioned by Jack on his Facebook, the room was lit up and he found himself surrounded by cops. Captain Brown uttered, "Jeremy Wilson, you're under arrest for murder of Susan Crawford and attempted murder of Jack O'Hara. You've right to remain silent. Anything you say can and will be used against you in the court of law. You have the right to an attorney. If you cannot afford an attorney, one will be provided for you. Do you understand the rights I have just read to you? With these rights in mind, do you wish to speak to me?"

Later in the year, with the testimony of the four arrested persons, the entire Meatloaf gang was brought down.

CHAPTER ELEVEN

Mystery Lovers' Forum

It had been a fortnight since the night of the gala. Captain Brown has already announced, “We’ve found Ms. Teressa LeRoy, safe and healthy. She’ll be in the public eye as soon as she feels comfortable.”

Since the announcement, this was the first mystery lovers’ meetup of the Simmons Public Library, online, like all fora of the library after outbreak of COVID-19 and subsequent lockdown. The librarian Mrs. Atkins declared, “Tonight we’ll hear from a real detective and his person of interest.”

Young and old, men and women cried to cheer Teressa as she appeared on their respective screens along with Nathan. After the audience became silent, Nathan told, “Let’s hear from the horse’s mouth.”

Teressa protested, “Terrible use of adage. Do I look like a horse?”

After laughter and responses died down, she began, “At the gala Susan realized that some of Meatloaf members were keeping an eye on her. I caught her in the lady’s room. Susan was perspiring heavily, nervous. To save Susan’s life, I exchanged my dress with Susan at the gala end. Yet the gang nabbed Susan when she was approaching the roadside parking to her car through the dimly lit paths of Library Park, towards sixtieth street across seventh avenue. I'm following her from a distance. Seeing Susan’s fate, I decided not to go home that night and the following nights. Because I heard the gang members mumbling, ‘Now we have to hush up the lady who gave the teacher the dress.’ I had my bedroll at my library locker, for the nights I sleep at Little Abode for Children shelter. I borrowed a lamp from the library store and some books. Started living in the attic of the library.”

Keith and Melissa reacted, “We saw you!”

Teressa apologized, “Yes. You did. I’m sorry that I had to turn off the motion sensors that night. To keep the library dark ... I needed to hide.”

Natalie asked, “Did you kick Detective Adams’? Did you hit him with some encyclopedia?”

Teressa blushed, then frowned, and replied, "Yah. I did. I thought that he was a gangster and would kill me. Why wouldn't I? He's unabashed by my attacks and he threw me to the bedroll and kept asking, 'Who are you? Why are you hiding here?' till I was turned face up and he recognized me. He apologized and showed his badge, bringing me to his home hiding in his car's trunk."

Someone asked, "Are you guys living happily ever after?"

Both Teressa and Nathan blushed. Then their eyes locked to each other. They forgot about their audience. They graduated to a long kiss.

Some exclaimed, "PDA. Ewe."

Some adored, "Awe!"

Stay In Touch

For updates on Advanced Readings, Beta Readings and Special Offers of books and to be part of my launch team sign up for my newsletter and stay up to date.

Also, you can follow me for updates on new releases on Amazon, Goodreads, Twitter, Facebook, Instagram, Pinterest, YouTube and on my blog Projection of Naught.

Praise For The Author

Street Facts: A Thriller Illuminating Darker Mysterious Sides of Streets (Kolkata Crime Cosmos Book 1)

This story is very short and succinct consisting of an event which causes a meeting between Shreeja, who finds a lone child crawling on the pavement and a woman who is a street beggar who rents the child from a gang who control the area, a bit like the Peachums in the Threepenny Opera. There is a lovely description of the child and the way they are fascinated by simple things, especially the tendency for very young children to taste things that aren't edible. I remember my son doing this but don't think I have ever read this in a story...although plenty of idiots guide to parenting books mention this trait, both endearing and concerning,of young explorers in life.I

The life of the beggar woman is revealed in a conversation between the two women and the way even begging is controlled by gangs of men who treat women as second class even though they are the ones doing most of the work. In a very short story misogyny in Indian society and the lengths people will go to to survive in poverty, ways we may find morally repugnant but are a necessity. These people are the invisible people that exist in all societies, the ones some may pretend not to see on leaving the supermarket or tram but who are real people and have real needs. Sometimes a connection between human beings is all that people need to make the day a little brighter.

I wanted to read more about these characters and their lives. How, if at all do I here people cover or is it just a chance meeting that reveals a something about t he society they live in. It reminded me of Tolstoy or Dickens, even Steven King, all of whom create these little vignettes within a longer story, sometimes with little relevance to the story other than the theme...except Steven King who then kills them off.

https://www.amazon.co.uk/product-reviews/B09LZ2XV4P

How to Steal a Pond: A Literary Fiction with Step by Step Lessons on Corruption

This is another look at the daily lives of people struggling to survive, doing their daily jobs, and learning their limits in forcing their agenda. Sometimes the best outcomes do not require violence but rather solid authority.

https://www.amazon.com/product-reviews/B07NKGLBKT

Maternal Might

Indian storyteller Sanhita Mukherjee spins a tale of female empowerment rooted in love for family and children in "Maternal Might." Bangladeshi mother Fatima becomes the family's breadwinner when she accepts a job as a surrogate for the first child of gay Israeli couple, Abel and Joshua. Mukherjee walks us through the characters' moral dilemma as they get involved in novel arrangements that defy societal norms. The story reinforces the power of money and status in creating opportunities that are not readily available to others.

The story is told from a pragmatic point of view: women living in poverty use their bodies in exchange for money so they can provide for their families. Fatima's job is not different from women's work involving taking care of other people's children. Attitudes about parenting meet modern science with the overlay of religious considerations. A Muslim woman has made the economic decision to bear the child of a Jewish couple in Nepal, a predominantly Buddhist country. Mukherjee boldly discusses these dynamics through dialogue.

In its current iteration, the story is a quick read, but it could easily be adapted to long-form prose. We understand the economic necessity of surrogacy for Fatima, and yet, there's much to explore in Abel and Joshua's decision to become parents. There are also plenty of opportunities to delve into the emotional lives of surrogate mothers. The reader is left wanting more, to explore how the decision of engaging in surrogate motherhood – as the birth mother or the expecting parents – affects everyone involved.

https://www.amazon.com/product-reviews/B09GL3HDGK

Sierra Papa Yankee

This author writes with an intimate knowledge of unrest, violence, and struggling in a different culture. His stories draw the reader into the scene. I would really like to read the entire book.

https://www.amazon.com/product-reviews/B09PBYMNM6

Little Abode for Children: A Mystery (American Small Town Mysteries Book 1)

"Little Abode for Children" is Book 1 of the American Small Town Mysteries series, written by Sanhita Mukherjee .... had an interesting storyline and some pretty great detective and police characters, as well a child characters. Little Abode for Children is the program started at a library by a librarian named Teressa for children who were either homeless, abused, or preyed upon by gang members. The lead detective, Nathan, reminded me of a 1940s/1950s Noir book/movie character. His boss, Captain Brown is a woman, because the text says "she". I liked Captain Brown's character because she was straight forward with her questions to the detective. I also liked the little children, Jack and Melissa.

https://www.amazon.com/product-reviews/B09HSQYBN2

Rescuing the Realm: A Fairytale (Banglish Fairy Tales Book 1)

I liked this story because it depicted the way that one brave person can change the future. A young girl who is low born, Pinky, uses her power to help her people.

https://www.amazon.co.uk/product-reviews/B09RBHXB8F

About Author

Starts her days with pots and pans. Then pushes 'Ls' after 'P's. Cooks stories with plots and plans.

Her mystery stories are solved by police detectives and fantasy stories include magic realism, sci-fi and epic world building.

Lives with her husband wherever he lives.

For updates on new releases sign in to her newsletter at : https://www.subscribepage.com/x8x3e1 AND Get a book.

Find Her on -

Goodreads: https://www.goodreads.com/author/dashboard?al_user=93464924-sanhita-mukherjee

Twitter: https://twitter.com/SanhitaMukherj6

Facebook: https://www.facebook.com/WrigglerSanhita2000s

Instagram: https://www.instagram.com/sanhitamukherjee3478/

YouTube: https://www.youtube.com/channel/UClyvXlZvL8Yvq2-NBCGeqKw

Blog : https://projectionofnaught.blogspot.com/

Pinterest: https://in.pinterest.com/tupur004

9 798889 861645

Printed by Libri Plureos GmbH in Hamburg,
Germany